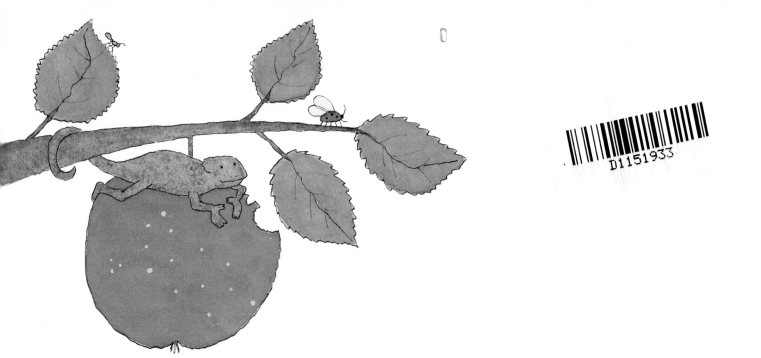

Little Chameleon

First published in the UK in 1998 by
Belitha Press Limited, London House,
Great Eastern Wharf, Parkgate Road,
London SW11 4NQ.

This edition first published in 1999

ISBN 1 85561 861 3 (paperback)
ISBN 1 85561 799 4 (hardback)

British Library Cataloguing in Publication Data
for this book is available from the British Library

Printed in China

Editor: Honor Head
Designer: Helen James
Calligraphy: Jan Barger

Little Chameleon

Jan Barger

Belitha Press

Little Chameleon was learning to change colours.

'Follow me,' said Mama Chameleon.
Mama ran up a brown tree.

Little Chameleon followed.
'Wrong colour,' said Mama.

Mama bit into a red apple.

Little Chameleon followed.
'Wrong colour,' said Mama.

Mama rode on a yellow hat.

Little Chameleon followed.
'Wrong colour,' said Mama.

Mama swung on some purple grapes.

Little Chameleon followed.
'Wrong colour,' said Mama.

Mama hid in a blue bowl.

Little Chameleon followed.
'Wrong colour,' said Mama.

Mama clung to a grey shoe.

Little Chameleon followed.
'Wrong colour,' said Mama.

Mama rested on a white
laundry basket.

*Little Chameleon darted about
changing from one colour…*

...to another.

'Well done!' said Mama.

Then Little Chameleon went to sleep.